Jinx

Allie

Liz

Drew

Puffin

Ragged Island Mysteries™

The Ship in a Bottle

by Emily Herman

Wright Group
McGraw-Hill

To Vin and Alice

The Ship in a Bottle
Text copyright © Emily Herman
Illustrations copyright © Wright Group/McGraw-Hill
Illustrations by Taylor Bruce

Ragged Island Mysteries™ is a trademark of The McGraw-Hill
Companies, Inc.

Wright Group/McGraw-Hill
19201 120th Avenue NE, Suite 100
Bothell, WA 98011
www.WrightGroup.com

Printed in the United States of America

10 9 8 7 6 5 4 3

ISBN: 0-322-01577-4
ISBN: 0-322-01648-7 (6-pack)

CONTENTS

CONTENTS

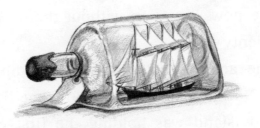

1

RAGGED ISLAND BREAK-IN

Allie Davies staggered into a clearing. Her arms were full of tools. She set them down and looked around her. Did she have all the supplies she needed?

Plywood? Over there. Leaning up against the spruce tree. Check.

Foam board and two-by-four studs? Next to the plywood. Check.

Tools? Sawhorses? Check and check.

Bicycle parts and a lobster trap?

Allie listened. Her friends Drew Ellis and Liz French would be bringing them any minute now. But even without them, Allie had plenty to do.

Allie and her friends were building a boat. Not just any boat. A racing boat. Ragged Island was holding the first ever Around the Harbor Lobster Trap Race. Allie planned to win.

She was worried, though. So many people on the island were entering. It wouldn't be easy to build the best boat.

She reached into her backpack and pulled out her plans. "It's a great design," she muttered to herself as she looked them over. "I hope it's allowed."

That was another problem. Allie didn't know the exact rules for the race. No one did. Not until 9:30 A.M. She checked her watch. Her friend Jinx should be picking the

rules up this exact minute.

But Allie didn't worry for long. She'd rather work. So she set the sawhorses up in the middle of the clearing.

It really was a perfect spot. Liz had discovered it just past her grandfather's cabin. For one thing, it had a beautiful view. Allie could stand in the middle of the

3

clearing and look out all the way across Mackerel Bay to the town of Bellport on the mainland. There were more important reasons why it was such a great spot, though. It was close to the shore. That would make it easy to launch their boat. It was near an electrical outlet, in case they needed to plug in power tools. And it was very, very private. Allie's design was original. She didn't want anyone to see what they were building.

At last she heard someone coming. Jinx?

No. She could hear Drew whistling. And Liz's wheelbarrow.

Liz pushed into the clearing first. She set the creaking wheelbarrow down. It had part of a bicycle in it. "Phew! Is that everything?"

"I hope so," Drew exclaimed. He dropped the lobster trap he was carrying. Then he gazed around the clearing. "It doesn't look like a boat yet."

"It will, though," Liz declared. "Let's call it the *Loon*. That's my favorite bird."

Allie thought about the loons she watched swimming and diving in Mackerel Bay all winter. She loved their lonely calls. "I like that name," she said.

"*Loony* might be a better name for it!" Drew pulled the bike part out of the wheelbarrow. "What is this for? Doesn't it have to be a sailboat?"

"Maybe to run a fan," Liz guessed. "In case there's no wind on the day of the race. Someone will have to pedal a huge fan to make wind."

Drew collapsed on the ground and groaned. "I'm afraid I know who that someone is."

"Actually," Allie said, "I don't know if we'll be able to use the pedals. If we can, I know we'll win. Where's Jinx?"

"You know Jinx," Liz said. "He's always late." Liz knew Jinx Harris well. They were cousins, next-door neighbors, and classmates, too.

"He's probably talking to someone," Drew added. He knew Jinx almost as well as Liz did.

"Rats! We're stuck until we get the rules," Allie said. "You should have gone, Liz."

"Can't we get started anyway?" Liz asked. "We know the boat has to include a lobster trap," Liz said. "And it needs a sail."

"Yes, we do know that much." Allie straightened out her tools as she talked. "But I need to know if it can also have a pedal-driven paddle."

"Why don't we just have a sail?" Liz asked. "You're a good sailor. You could probably beat everyone anyway."

"I don't know," Allie said. "There's a lot of competition. I want the prize."

"What's so great about the prize?" Drew asked.

The prize was a ship in a bottle and the winner's name on a plaque.

"The winner doesn't even get to keep the bottle," Liz said.

"The winner gets to keep it for a week," Allie said. She sighed. "I'd love to get that ship in a bottle. Even if only for a week."

"How come?" Liz asked.

"It's amazing," Allie said. "There's a little carved boat inside a bottle, with sails and rigging. It's absolutely perfect. But it's much too big to fit through the narrow neck of the bottle. And no one can reach into the bottle to put the masts and sails in place. How does anyone make a ship in a bottle?"

Drew shrugged. "It's a mystery, all right."

7

"There must be a trick," Allie said. "The bottle comes apart. Or there's a special tool. I bet if I could examine the bottle closely for a week, I could figure it out."

"You could go see it in the museum," Liz reminded her.

"Right. With Mrs. Matthews warning me not to touch." Allie picked up her block plane. She handed it to Drew. She set a two-by-four on the sawhorses. "Okay. Even without Jinx we can get something done. Drew, you start planing the mast down. We want it to be smooth."

Drew saluted her. "Aye, aye, Captain." He looked at the block plane. It had a neon green splotch on it. All of Allie's tools had neon paint on them. "Pretty bright," he said. "Guess you won't lose many tools that way."

"What should I do?" Liz asked.

"We'll need a rudder to steer the *Loon*,"

8

Allie directed. "I've traced it on the plywood. Would you cut it out with the jigsaw?"

Once Liz and Drew were set up, Allie started taking the bicycle apart.

Allie was absolutely happy. For one thing, everything smelled so good. She breathed in deeply, then sorted all the smells: wood shavings, sawdust, bicycle grease, and mostly fresh island air, filled with salt and seaweed and pine needles baking in the sun.

For another thing, she and her friends were building something. Allie didn't mind talking, but making something was so much better.

Best of all, Allie was filled with excitement. She loved contests. She loved coming up with new ideas, trying her hardest, and doing her best. Win or lose, she always learned something, but she especially loved to win.

The clearing was quieter once Liz had finished cutting out the rudder. Now she was sanding it.

Drew asked, "Who thought up this race anyway?"

"I know that much," Liz said. "Gramp told me. A guy named T. S. Lang. He usually comes here every summer, but this year he'll be away. Maybe next year, too." Liz raised her eyebrows. "Can you believe he makes up crossword puzzles for a living?"

"And puts ships in bottles," Allie added.

"That's his hobby," Liz said.

"How come no one told me about him? I'd have gone to see him and asked him how he did it," Allie said.

"And he wouldn't have told," Liz replied.

Drew said, "Like a magician."

"Right," Liz said. "They never tell their secrets."

Allie could understand that. "I'd rather figure it out on my own anyway," Allie said. "So where's Jinx? We can't do much more without him."

Before Liz or Drew could reply, they heard crashing in the bushes.

"Sounds like a moose," Drew said.

The noise came closer and closer until Jinx broke into the clearing.

"In the nick of time! We need the rules before..." Allie would have gone on, but Jinx held up his hand. Then he panted and doubled over, trying to catch his breath.

"You should have gone for the rules, Liz," Drew said. "You're in the best shape for running."

"That...wouldn't have...mattered," Jinx gasped. "No one...would have been...any quicker. It would have taken anyone...that long to get...through."

11

"Get through what?" Liz exclaimed.

"The police," Jinx answered.

"You're joking," Drew said.

"Hey guys, I'm serious," Jinx said. "Sheriff Greenwood was talking to Mrs. Tinkham. I couldn't exactly barge in and ask for the rules to the race."

"This had better not be an excuse because you forgot the rules," Allie said.

Jinx reached into his pocket and pulled out a wadded-up paper. "Right here." He handed the rules to Allie. "But listen. There was a break-in at the Tinkhams'. Can you believe it? On Ragged Island?"

"The store?" Liz asked.

"No, their house. Mr. Tinkham had already left for the store. When Mrs. T. came down, she found a broken windowpane in her living room."

"What was taken?" Liz asked.

"That was what was really weird," Jinx said. "Nothing. You know Mrs. Tinkham. She has all that old furniture."

"Yeah, and paintings by Ragged Island artists," Liz said. "Some of those are valuable—or will be someday."

"And a million knick knacks," Drew said.

13

"Sometimes I help cart boxes to her house from the ferry. She gets a batch almost every week."

"So maybe it was vandalism," Allie said. "You know. A kid threw a rock?"

"No, they figured someone went in. Mrs. T. noticed one thing was disturbed. You know the prize for the race?"

"Someone took the ship in the bottle?" Allie asked.

"Someone tried. Mrs. Tinkham said it arrived yesterday in a big box. She had unpacked it. Then she closed the lid and left the box in her living room," Jinx said. "This morning, the box had been upended. The stuffing had been dumped out. Let's go back. I want to see what's going on."

"Wait a sec." Allie opened the page of rules. She skimmed down them, then smiled up at her friends. "We can use the bike pedals," she said.

"Can we take the time to go to town?" Liz asked.

Allie looked around at the job they'd started. "We have a lot more to do, but we're in great shape," she said. "Besides, a robbery on Ragged Island is a big deal. Especially one connected to the race's prize. What could possibly make it so valuable that someone would break into a house for it?"

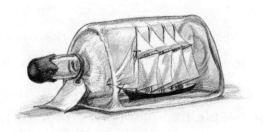

2

SPYING ON THE COMPETITION

Tinkhams' General Store had been the
center of Ragged Island for generations. The
building was old. The windows were small.
The floor was uneven. But everyone visited
the store at one time or another. In the
winter, when it was too stormy to fish,
people played cribbage around a potbellied
stove. In the summer, the shelves were full
of fancy cookies and cheeses, especially for
summer people. Mr. Tinkham took care of

the business. Mrs. Tinkham took care of the talking.

The store was crowded by the time Allie got to town. She could hear Mrs. Tinkham's loud voice as she discussed the break-in. Other people had plenty of comments, too.

"Who would have done a thing like that?"

"Probably kids on a dare."

"Must have been a stranger. Anyone from around here knows to just walk through the front door."

"I'm going to start locking my door at night. I'll tell you that."

"Foam peanuts everywhere," Mrs. Tinkham said. "I already had them out once, looking for a letter about the scholarship money T. S. Lang promised us."

"He sent a check?" someone asked.

"Not in that box," Mrs. Tinkham said. "Just the ship and the rules." She sighed.

"Sheriff took the box as evidence, but he didn't think to clean up all the packing for me."

By now Allie had squeezed her way into the store behind Jinx. She couldn't see Liz or Drew anywhere. She was close enough to the counter to see the prize bottle itself.

It wasn't an everyday kind of bottle. It was maybe ten inches long. It had a narrow neck and rested on its side. She could see the ship, but not very clearly. She worked her way closer.

"What is this island coming to?" someone said.

"I'm certainly glad I put the bottle in a safe place," Mrs. Tinkham said. "Though why anyone would try to take it I don't know."

Allie noticed there was a tag tied around the neck. She wanted to get even closer, but elbows kept getting in her way. She whispered to Jinx, "Do you think you could find out what that tag says?"

"Why?" Jinx asked.

"Something is strange here," Allie answered. "Why would anyone want to steal this bottle? Maybe the tag has a clue."

Jinx nodded. Jinx was short and wiry enough to squeeze through gaps in the crowd. But even he couldn't get close. Finally he called out, "Excuse me, Mrs. Tinkham, what does the tag say?"

Mrs. Tinkham looked annoyed at the interruption. Still, Jinx had asked politely. The crowd hushed a little, waiting to hear. So she lifted the bottle carefully, adjusted the tag, and read, "For the people of Ragged Island, a jewel in the middle of Mackerel Bay."

Allie thought the words over. She didn't

see any clue there. Then she listened to the comments around her.

"Oh, that's nice."

"He's going to miss being here for the next few years."

"Hear his wife has a great job over in Greece. And he can make up his crosswords anywhere."

Jinx once again appeared at her side. "Did that help?"

21

Allie shrugged. It just sounded like a gift tag to her.

"Let's get out of here and find the others," Jinx said.

"After all, we have a boat to build!" Allie said.

They found Drew and Liz, as well as Lauren McBride, another classmate, sitting on the stoop of the ice-cream shop.

"If anyone has money I can borrow, I'll treat," Jinx said.

"No money, but information," Drew said.

"About the bottle?" Allie asked.

"About the race," Drew said. "Word on the street is that this is a hot race. There are twenty entries altogether, but only four or five are likely winners."

"We made that list," Liz added.

"My brother's entering," Lauren said. "Owen's building something with Daniel."

Allie nodded. She had seen her younger brother Daniel making plans with Owen McBride at the kitchen table when she left that morning. "Who else?" Allie asked.

"I know Tony's entering," Jinx said. "He asked Dad if he could build an entry during off hours and Dad said okay." Jinx's father ran Rich's Fix-It, a repair shop on the island. Twenty-year-old Tony Pucci was his helper. Tony had clever hands and lots of patience.

"He'll have the use of every tool imaginable. I wonder what he's making." Allie looked at Jinx. "Have you seen it? What are we up against?"

Jinx held up his hands. "I have no idea. If I show up in that shop, Dad puts me to work. Let someone else check it out."

"I'll go," Liz said. "But he's not the only competitor. There's Mark Mason."

"He's just a summer visitor," Jinx said.

"Maybe so, but he's a great sailor," Allie said. "He used to win lots of the races in Mackerel Bay."

"Isn't he going to college now?" Liz asked.

"Uh-huh," Lauren said. "He studies mechanical engineering."

"Why doesn't he have a summer job somewhere else?" Jinx complained.

"This is great. Competition to keep us on our toes," Allie said. But she was getting anxious to get back to the clearing. All this talk wasn't building a boat!

"Speaking of competition," Lauren said, "Mark was at Tinkhams'. You should have seen his face when he heard Tony had named his boat the *Maggie*."

"How come?" Liz asked.

"Maggie Haswell was Mark's girlfriend last summer," Lauren replied. "I guess she likes Tony now."

"Maggie isn't even around this summer," Allie said. "I should know. She used to be our baby-sitter. This summer she's working off-island. Mom was desperate for a while. She had a terrible time finding a new sitter." She stood up and faced her friends. "Come on, guys. We have work to do."

"Wait," Drew said. "There's one more major competitor,"

"Who's that?" Allie asked.

"I don't know their names," Drew answered. "They're renting the old Lang guest cottage for this month."

"But they have a good entry?" Allie asked.

"That's what we heard. Right, Liz?" Drew asked.

Liz nodded.

Jinx groaned. "They're probably rocket

scientists from NASA. Hey, Allie. I know we have to go back soon. But let's have a quick look at the competition. Liz could go to my dad's fix-it shop to check Tony's boat."

Liz nodded.

"Drew, could you see what ideas Mark Mason brought back from college?" Jinx asked.

"Sure. As soon as I move some boxes for Mrs. Tinkham," Drew said. He was big and strong and often did yard work and odd jobs for the Tinkhams.

"And Allie and I will go do a quick check of the people at Langs' cottage," Jinx continued.

"But isn't that spying?" Lauren asked.

"Spying?" Allie considered the idea. "We don't really need to spy. We have a great plan. I think it's okay to see what we're up against."

Jinx and Allie jogged past the school and up to where Moody Road met Cross Street. The Lang cottage was near the corner, but not right on the road. They wouldn't be able to see much. Not unless they walked up the driveway.

Now that they were there, Allie felt more like a spy. "What do you think?" she asked. "Do we walk right in?"

"You still have the rules for the race, don't you?" Jinx asked.

Allie patted her pocket. "Uh-huh."

"We can always offer them a copy of the rules," Jinx said.

"Sounds like a plan," Allie said. She took the rules out and started smoothing them across her stomach as they walked down the driveway.

"Should we go up to the front door and knock?" Jinx asked.

27

There was no sign of a boat in the front yard. "They must be working out back," Allie said. "Or maybe no one is home." She edged around the corner of the cottage.

The first thing she saw was a big blue tarp. It was like a wall. Allie couldn't see around it. "That's funny," Allie wondered out loud. "This tarp isn't here to keep the rain out."

"Do you suppose it's hiding the boat?" Jinx whispered.

Allie shrugged. "I don't know why else." She moved a little closer. She peered around the edge of the tarp. All she could see was another layer of tarp. "They must have an incredible design."

Jinx was right beside her. "It couldn't be as clever as your pedal design. Could it?"

Allie got down on her hands and knees. She lifted the tarp away from the ground and stuck her head under it.

"What can you see?" Jinx whispered.

Allie didn't say anything. She was too busy looking. And trying to figure out what she was looking at.

She saw legs of sawhorses, lots of extension cords tangled like orange and yellow snakes, sawdust, wood chips, and a narrow, streamlined hull, shaped...

"Hey!" That was a kid's voice. It wasn't coming from behind the tarp. It was coming from the house.

"What is it, Tye?" a man asked. His voice also came from the house.

Allie started to stand. Then she realized she was inside the tarp. She backed out, then stood, brushing sawdust off her knees. She also smoothed the crumpled race rules she was holding. But before she could say anything, a boy burst out of the back door.

He had blond hair, was maybe a year or two older than Allie, and was much taller. He looked like someone who lifted weights for exercise.

"What are you doing? Spying on us?" he demanded.

Jinx snatched the rules away from Allie. He held them out. "We wanted to make sure..." he started.

"Did they get behind the tarp?" the man said. "Did they see anything?"

"If they did, they'll be sorry," the boy cried. He charged down the back steps. "I'll make sure of that."

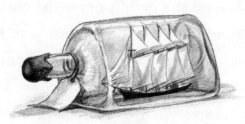

3

BLAMED

Jinx gave Allie a shove. "Get going," he
yelled. "You cut through Cathedral Woods. I'll
take the Ice Pond route."

They knew the island well. As fast as
the boy ran, he couldn't catch
them. He must have chosen to
chase Allie, because she heard
him thrashing through the
woods behind her. She ducked
onto a different path. Once she
was sure she had lost him, she
doubled back toward the work site.

She felt funny as she walked along. Guilty. Maybe she hadn't been just checking the competition. Maybe Lauren was right. Maybe it had been spying. But how come the people had been so mad?

Jinx caught up with her just before she got to Rocky Point Road. He stopped to catch his breath. "Phew," he said. "I'm getting my exercise today."

"Okay, " Allie said. "We shouldn't have been there. But is it my imagination, or did those people overreact?"

"After all, we were just bringing them the race rules," Jinx added.

"Right. So how come they got mad so fast?"

Jinx shrugged. "You know how some people love their privacy. They come to Ragged Island just so they don't get bothered by other people."

"I guess." Allie shook her head. "Either that, or they have an incredible boat design. I couldn't see very much."

"They're from Ohio," Jinx said.

Allie looked at him in amazement. "How do you know that? Their accents?"

"Their car. License plates," he answered.

"Good eye, Jinx," Allie said. "Well. Back to work." She held out her hand. "Let's see the rules."

"I don't have them," Jinx said.

"But didn't you take them?" Allie tried to remember. "When the summer people started yelling?"

"You're right. I did." Jinx held out his empty hands. "But I don't have them now. I dropped them during the chase."

Allie laughed. "Maybe we did give them the rules after all. Rats. I need to read them more carefully."

"I'll go get another set." Jinx started jogging back to town. Then he yelled over his shoulder, "I'll find Drew and Liz, too."

"No lingering, though," Allie warned. "We only have a day and a half to finish this thing." She turned onto Rocky Point Road, toward Gramp LaPlante's house.

Allie didn't mind having time to herself. As the oldest of five kids, she was never alone at home. And it gave her time to think over her boat plans again. With such tough competition, maybe she should make changes. She could reshape the hull a little, to make it sleeker. But not so much that the *Loon* could tip over! Maybe her design was perfect the way it was.

Then she started to think about the ship in the bottle. She hadn't seen it clearly enough. The bottle was beautiful. It was almost triangular. Maybe the bottle did come apart. There had to be some trick, because the ship was too big to fit through the neck. It had at least two masts and old-fashioned square sails. She hadn't been able to see more than that. It was an amazing bottle, but why would anyone want to steal it?

Her feet found their way toward the work area. But something quieted her feet and stopped her mind from daydreaming.

What was it? A noise? Maybe a twig cracking? Or the crunch of dried moss? Allie hesitated just a moment, then rushed to the work area.

No one was there. Nothing looked out of place. The boat was exactly as she had left it.

Maybe the sound had been made by Drew. Or Liz. Maybe one of them had come to the work site. Since no one was there, that person had left again to go looking for the others. Except...

Hadn't she straightened her tools? Allie scanned the tools and supplies, matching them with what she knew should be there.

Hadn't she put everything back on the ground before they left? So much had happened this morning that it was hard to keep track.

A sudden sound stopped her again. Definitely a footstep in the distance. Lots of footsteps. Voices, too. It sounded as if Jinx had found Drew and Liz. Allie walked toward the path to meet them. But one look at the serious expressions on their faces stopped her.

"What's wrong?"

"Well, the good news is we found the name of the people in Langs' cottage," Jinx said.

"Okay. Who are they?" Allie asked.

"Their last name is Selfridge," Liz said.

"And they're out to get you and Jinx," Drew added. "That's the bad news."

"That's ridiculous," Allie said. "How

would they even know us?"

"They saw us, remember?" Jinx said.

"They were asking who the Japanese kid was," Liz said.

"Oh," Allie said. She didn't often think about how different she looked from most islanders. She had been born in Korea. The Davies family had adopted her when she was a baby. "I don't suppose anyone straightened the Selfridges out about my background," she said. "But why are they out to get us?"

"You aren't going to believe this, Allie," Jinx said, "but they're saying we were going to wreck their boat!"

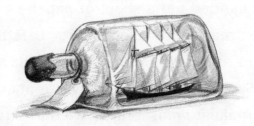

4

NOISES IN THE NIGHT

"That's ridiculous!" Allie repeated.

"You know that," Liz said. "And we know that. But some people are pretty upset."

"Mrs. Tinkham?" Allie guessed.

Drew nodded. "It seems Lauren mentioned you were checking out the competition."

"What?" Allie was indignant. "It's not like we needed to see what everyone else was doing. We have a great design of our own."

She looked at Jinx. "Did you bring another set of the rules?"

Jinx handed her a sheet of paper.

Allie read the rules more carefully. "'Lobster trap, old or new...must have a sail...' See, it does say we may use another way to make it go as long as we don't use a motor." She looked up happily. "We'll win with pedal power!"

"But what about the Selfridges?" Liz asked.

"And Mrs. Tinkham," Drew added. "I got roped into helping her with another box of junk. She warned me that if anyone does anything to wreck this race, she will disqualify that team on the spot."

"We didn't do anything," Allie insisted. "No one can blame us for looking. And now, we've got a job to do!"

Allie was a great commanding officer.

42

She had to be. She had three younger brothers and a little sister. Her father and mother both worked. They also were on a million committees. And they loved to give parties. Someone had to be in charge of everyday things. Allie was that someone. And when she had a plan of her own, she knew exactly how to get the job done. By the time the six o'clock ferry horn sounded, their boat was taking shape.

Drew stretched back, looking at the sky. "Phew! What a day!" he said.

43

"This is really shaping up, though," Jinx said. "I love this seat!" They'd taken the wire lobster trap apart and put it together again a different way. Now it looked like a comfortable chair. Jinx sat in it and leaned back. He pretended to pedal. "Feels great!"

"A prize-winning design," Liz added.

"I hope so." Allie looked at the entry critically. Then her expression changed. She was remembering the noises she'd heard near the boat.

"You look worried," Drew said.

"I was thinking," Allie said. "I hope nothing happens to this boat." She sighed. "Oh well, I'm sure it'll be safe. We can get back to work on it at first light tomorrow."

"Which comes at four A.M. these days," Jinx complained.

"We only have thirty-eight hours left," Allie said. "We need every second."

Jinx laughed. "You have to let us go home to eat now and then. We need to keep up our strength. Come on, Drew. Let's get out of here before she figures out another way to give us blisters."

As the two boys left the work area, Liz said, "I can keep working with you until dark. It's The Beautiful Marla's turn to take care of things." Liz's mom ran the Rocky Point Bed and Breakfast. Liz and her sister, Marla, helped out a lot. Actually Liz helped out a lot. The Beautiful Marla often came up with other things to do. Like brushing her hair.

"You get a night off? That's great!" Allie exclaimed. "Hey! We could camp out tonight. Do you want to?"

"Here? To protect the boat?" Liz nodded. "Brilliant!"

Allie puttered on the boat while Liz ran

home to get permission and camping supplies. Then, while Liz set up camp, Allie raced home to get her stuff.

"How's your boat coming?" she asked Daniel as she jogged past him on her way back to camp.

"Great," he said, "except Owen had to go home." Daniel had a nail in one hand, a hammer in the other, and was keeping a board in place by leaning against it. "It's hard working on my own."

"I know. I'd help, but I have to get back to my boat," Allie said. She did pause to look over Daniel's progress.

He'd done a pretty good job. It looked like an upside-down table so far. There were a lot of bent nails and some of the boards hadn't been cut exactly square. But it looked as if it would float. And it might even hold together for the whole race. "Impressive, bro," she said.

Daniel didn't even look up. "Dad helped a little with the cutting," he said. "And Mom did some of the hammering."

"I like the shape," she said. "And the way you've got the railing...Hey!" A splash of green caught her eye. "That's my wrench!"

"Oh!" Daniel raced over to it. The board he had been leaning against crashed to the ground. He snatched the wrench up and handed it to her. "We just borrowed it. Just for a sec. You can have it back."

Allie put her hands on her hips. "You know neon green tools are my tools!" she scolded. "I let you use them when you ask."

"Yeah, right," Daniel muttered. "Anyway, you weren't there to ask."

"And what were you doing at our building site?" Allie went on. "We wanted complete privacy. That's why..."

"Whoa! Cool it, dudes."

Allie turned. It was Mark Mason. He was leaning against the maple tree, watching.

"What are you doing here?" Daniel asked. "Spying?"

Mark raised his eyebrows at Allie. "I'm not the spy, dude."

Allie glared back at him.

"Hey, if you hold that board, I'll hammer for you," Mark offered to Daniel. "I'm looking for Maggie. She here?"

"She's not baby-sitting for us this year," Daniel said. "I don't think she's on Ragged Island at all this summer. Is she, Allie?"

Allie shrugged. "Maybe weekends." She remembered how much Mark hung around Maggie the summer before without doing anything to help out. She was glad Maggie was going with Tony now instead of Mark. "Look, Daniel. I have to get back. Good luck on your boat. Ask next time, okay?"

Daniel waved and turned his attention to Mark. Allie smiled to herself as she jogged back to camp. It never mattered to Daniel who he was talking to, as long as he was talking. But then her smile faded. She was no spy! No matter what Mark thought.

She forgot all about Mark Mason once she got back to the boatyard. For one thing, the *Loon* was looking even better than she'd remembered. For another, Liz had brought some of her mother's famous blueberry muffins and a big thermos of chowder for supper.

They decided not to have a campfire. But they were glad when Liz's grandfather, Roland LaPlante, came down at dusk to say good night. He didn't need a campfire to tell stories.

"Pull up a rock, Mr. LaPlante," Allie said.

"Quite a contraption you're putting together," Gramp said. He gave the pedal a spin. "That will take some pumping. Who's got the legs for that?"

"Drew is going to pedal and Allie's going

to sail, Gramp," Liz said. "Jinx and I will be cheering from dry land."

"Only two people can be on the boat," Allie explained. "The rules are quite thorough."

Gramp chuckled. "That's just like T. S."

"T. S.?" Allie asked.

"T. S. Lang. He sure does like to get people's heads spinning." Gramp shook his head. "His puzzles set people weeping. They call him up, begging for hints. He just shakes his head. I beat him at checkers, though."

"Well, Allie, I guess we'd better win that bottle," Liz said. "It sounds like you'd never get Mr. Lang to tell you how he put the ship into it."

"He'll teach you, though," Gramp said. "He was helping one boy last summer. Don't know who."

"When's he coming back?" Allie asked.

"Not for a year or two. Wife's got a good job overseas. I told him he could come back and play checkers with me over the summer, but he said he rented both houses. I know some artist fellow has his island house year round. Some relatives must have his other house. It's somewhere in Ohio, I think. Cincinnati, maybe?" He got up to leave. "Going to miss him. I won't be the only one. More than one islander's made it through a hard winter thanks to his help. Almost every year he throws a little something into the island's pot."

"Hey, I remember seeing his name in books in the library," Allie said.

"He paid for most everything in the library," Gramp said. "Probably a good thing he's gone for a year or two. Help us stand on our own two feet. Still, I'll miss beating him at checkers." Gramp started up the path to his cabin. "Sleep well now," he called softly.

"I think your grandfather likes to win as much as I do," Allie said.

"At checkers anyway." Liz got a sudden idea. "You should play him sometime, Allie. He always beats me."

"That would be fun," Allie said, but she didn't seem to be paying attention to what she was saying.

"What is it, Allie?" Liz asked

"I wish Chief had come with you," she said. Chief was Jinx's dog. "I keep hearing sounds."

"It's just Gramp heading back to his house," Liz suggested.

"Maybe. Besides," Allie reminded herself, "the other noises came from Daniel. He borrowed my wrench."

"Maybe," Liz muttered. She was holding

absolutely still, listening. "Now I have a funny feeling someone's out there."

"I don't hear anything," Allie whispered.

"Except mosquitoes," Liz replied.

It was a perfect summer night. There weren't that many mosquitoes. Dogs barked in the distance. A car drove by, heading toward town. Water lapped at the beach below them. The air smelled of roses.

Allie leaned back on her sleeping bag and looked at the stars. She recognized familiar constellations. Then she started wondering. "I'm thinking about that bottle," Allie said softly. "Someone actually broke into a house looking for it."

"Actually, we don't know that," Liz said. "They could have been looking for something else. Mrs. T. said something about scholarship money Mr. Lang promised. Maybe that's what the thief was looking for."

"Maybe," Allie agreed. "But about that bottle. If Mr. Lang is such a puzzle nut..."

"What did the tag say again?" Liz asked.

Allie had a great memory. "For the people of Ragged Island, a jewel in the middle of Mackerel..." she quoted.

"Shhh!" Liz hushed. "What's that?"

They listened. They listened so hard they stopped breathing. Nothing.

Then they heard a sneeze.

Then a branch snapped.

"Someone really is out there sneaking around," Allie said. "Let's find out who!"

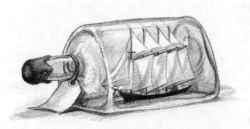

5
MIDNIGHT INTRUDERS

Allie and Liz charged toward the sound. At first it seemed to come from the woods, but then they heard someone laugh. That sound came from Gramp LaPlante's barn. Then they saw a beam of light. Somebody had a flashlight. Two people with flashlights! Two different voices shouting! And a dog barking! Someone called, "Go get him, Chief!"

Someone with Jinx's voice.

And someone else with Drew's voice, very close, very out of breath, was saying, "I'll check the boat."

And then Drew ran right into Liz!

Allie stopped short in front of him. "What are you doing here?" she asked, hands on her hips.

Jinx stepped out of the shadows beside Drew. "What are you two doing here?" he retorted. Chief sat down beside him and scratched.

"We're camping out by the boat," Allie said. "To keep an eye on it."

Jinx laughed. "Great minds think alike, I guess. Drew and I figured we should do the same thing. We just got a later start."

Drew helped Liz up. "You okay?" he asked.

Liz brushed herself off. "Sure."

"You're camping out? Where are your

sleeping bags?" Allie asked.

"I dropped them when I heard you sneeze," Drew said. "Back by Gramp's garden, I think."

"We didn't sneeze," Allie said. "You did."

Jinx looked at Drew. "Neither of us sneezed." He dropped his voice. "Could someone else be in the woods?"

"A spy!" Allie hissed.

They all held silent for a few seconds to see if this was true. It was quiet, except for the mosquitoes.

And some quick rustling sounds.

Then a thud and a muffled groan.

"There is someone else!" Allie whispered.

"Let's get him!" Jinx shouted.

Jinx and Liz knew the area best. They charged into the woods. Allie and Drew weren't far behind. They aimed in a slightly different direction and burst through the trees onto the road. Once there, they peered up and down it, looking for a shadow out of place.

But suddenly Allie realized they'd left the boat unattended. "I'm heading back," she whispered to Drew. "This might be a trap. No one is guarding the boat."

As she made her way back to their camp, she heard crashing sounds in the woods coming from more than one direction. "Everyone must have split up," she thought. Slowly the sounds grew more and more faint. At last she was left with only night noises and her thoughts.

This was getting serious. What started out as a fun contest for a hot summer day was turning more dangerous. Someone wanted that bottle enough to break into the Tinkhams' house. No one ever broke into houses on the island. Well, almost never.

And now people were spying on other people's boats. Allie felt a little funny about that. She had tried to do it herself. It hadn't seemed wrong at the time. But now... She didn't like the feeling of an unknown person creeping around her boat.

Allie knew she must be tired because her thoughts kept going around in circles, but she was too keyed up to sleep. It seemed as if the others were taking ages getting back.

At last she heard a mourning dove call that sounded suspicious. Sometimes Jinx made that sound as a signal.

"Jinx?" Allie said softly.

"Yo!" Jinx answered.

"Are the others with you?" Allie asked.

"We've just regrouped." Jinx collapsed on the ground. Liz and Drew were right behind him. "Man! We've been all over the island tonight!"

"Did you see anything?" Allie asked.

"Nothing," Liz said.

"We swung by a few other work areas," Drew said. "No one was working. No lights were on. Nothing!"

"Well, that's good!" Allie said. "I was getting worked up about this."

"We can hunt around for signs of intruders in the morning," Jinx said. It was hard to understand him. He was yawning too hard.

The yawn was catching. Before long, he and Drew had stumbled back to find their sleeping bags. Allie and Liz fell asleep guarding the boat.

Allie woke at dawn. She slipped out of her sleeping bag and looked around. Nothing was out of place. Then she headed for where she'd heard noises the night before.

Probably there were really great trackers

in the world. They'd know which branches had been broken by a deer, by a spy, or by four chasers. Allie couldn't. She found footprints, but couldn't really tell them apart. She thought she saw a different tread—kind of like a deer print, only solid— but it was hard to tell.

She was standing quietly, looking at the ground, when Liz joined her. "Anything?"

"Does this look like a track?" asked Allie.

Liz crouched down and looked closely. "Like a narrow heel print?"

"That's what I thought. Only it could be just a deer," Allie said.

"I'm glad we guarded the boat, just in case. Listen, I have to help Ma this morning," Liz told her. "I'll probably be able to get away by noon."

"That'll be great," Allie said. "We're mostly done."

"The *Loon* is a great boat," Liz assured her.

When Jinx and Drew got up, they both had things to do first thing in the morning, too. Allie was happy enough to work alone. She had to make the pedal-paddle perfect! She expected to have two or three hours of quiet time.

She barely got fifteen minutes!

She heard Jinx before she saw him.

"This secret spot is getting to be a highway," she complained.

Jinx interrupted her before she could go on. "It's a good thing we stayed here last night," he said. "Tony's boat was wrecked last night."

"In your dad's shop?" Allie asked.

"Behind it," answered Jinx. "That's where he was working on it."

Allie was shocked. "Can he fix it?"

Jinx shook his head. "It's ruined. Like someone took a pry bar and took it all to pieces."

"Who did it?" asked Allie. "Are there any clues?"

"Don't get all innocent on me, Allie Davies!" Mrs. Tinkham stormed into the clearing, holding what looked like a stick in her hand.

Allie looked from her to Jinx.

Jinx stared right back at her. "She thinks we did it."

"But we didn't," Allie protested.

Mrs. Tinkham held out her hand. In it was a pry bar. On the handle was a splotch of neon green paint.

"Is this familiar?" she asked icily.

Allie didn't have to look. She knew right off. The green paint helped her keep track of all her tools. But she scanned her tools,

just to make sure. No pry bar. "Where was it?"

"Among the splinters of Tony's boat," Mrs. Tinkham answered.

"We'd never do that!" Allie insisted.

"Drew tells me that YOUR boat wasn't hurt," Mrs. Tinkham stated.

"That's true," Allie said.

"We decided to camp out to protect it," Jinx added.

66

"And why would you ever think it needed protecting?" Mrs. Tinkham asked.

"I thought I heard someone near it yesterday after..." Allie began.

"And was this after you were seen at the Selfridges?" Mrs. Tinkham interrupted.

"We were just..." Allie tried to explain.

"And I understand you were all over the island last night." Mrs. Tinkham was very angry.

"We heard sounds near our boat, so we chased..." said Jinx.

Mrs. Tinkham's voice rang out clearly. "I warned you about this. No one who damages another person's boat has the right to take part in this race." She glared sternly at Allie and Jinx. "You will not be allowed to enter tomorrow."

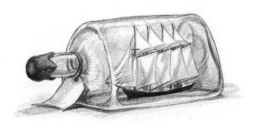

6

THE WRECKED SHIP

"But we didn't..." said Jinx.

"We wouldn't..." said Allie.

Mrs. Tinkham held up her hand to stop Jinx and Allie from saying anything. "Mr. Lang would be disgusted by this. He loves challenges, but he always plays fair. Now I warned you already about interfering with other people's boats."

"Mrs. Tinkham, we would never, ever destroy someone else's work," Allie insisted.

But she was talking to Mrs. Tinkham's stiff back. They watched as she walked out of sight.

"She didn't listen," Allie said as she turned back to Jinx.

"She never does. Haven't you noticed?" Jinx gave an unhappy laugh. "She likes to talk more."

Allie sank down beside the unfinished boat. Jinx sat beside her. "Now what?" he asked.

For some reason, Allie's mind wasn't working too well this morning. It had been so full of plans and tools and materials and how to put things together so she could win. She had to empty all that out, just to breathe.

Finally she could take a deep breath. "Okay. We didn't do it, right?"

"Right," Jinx said.

Allie thought about what to do next. "So we need to figure out who did," she said slowly. "And why."

"And then we'll be able to finish the boat and take part in the race," Jinx added.

Allie looked over her boat again. She knew there wasn't much time for all that. She sighed. "Oh, well."

"You know what confuses me?" Jinx asked. "What is it about the bottle that makes people want it so much? First they try to steal it. Now they are wrecking boats."

"We could find Mr. Lang's phone number and call him," Allie said.

"Except he never gives answers to his puzzles," Jinx said.

"Wait a minute. Do you think the message on the tag is a code?" Allie grabbed a pencil off the sawhorse and started writing on a scrap of plywood. "Let's see. 'For the people of Ragged Island, a jewel in the middle of Mackerel Bay.'"

She wrote down "Ftporiajitmomb." She tried to read it forward and backward. "Okay. He didn't use a simple code. Not the first letter of each word."

"Try the last letter," Jinx suggested.

Allie wrote "reefdd," then stopped. "You know what I want to do first?"

Jinx shook his head.

"Go see Tony," she said. "I want him to know we didn't do it."

When Jinx and Allie got there, Tony was alone in the shop, taking apart an outboard motor. He looked up for a second. When he saw who it was, he quickly bent over his work.

"We heard about what happened," Jinx said.

"Mrs. Tinkham thinks we did it, but we

never would," Allie blurted.

"It was your pry bar," Tony said. He wouldn't look at them.

"It was my pry bar. I can't explain that," Allie said. "But you know I'd never destroy someone's work."

"I wish I could believe that for sure," Tony replied. "It doesn't seem like something you guys would do. But who else would do it?"

Allie hated the way she was feeling. Everyone always had believed her before. They had listened to her and respected her ideas. And now she was not even trusted! "I wish we could prove it to you!" she exclaimed.

Tony tapped the carburetor. "Guess you'll have to," he said.

"Would you mind if we looked at your boat?" Jinx asked.

Tony shrugged. "It's your father's shop. How can I say no?"

Allie and Jinx walked behind the shop. Tony followed, as if he couldn't trust them out of his sight.

Not that there was much anyone could do to make things worse. They stared at the mess of splintered wood and foam board chunks.

Tony sighed. "It was a sweet design."

Allie walked all around the wreck. It made her stomach hurt. How could anyone do this? Tony always did careful work. He had clever ideas, too. She noticed a piece of the bottom of the boat. Its shape surprised her. "How come you made the keel so sharp?" she asked.

"I got that from something Mr. Lang showed me last year."

"You know Mr. Lang?" Allie asked.

"Yup. He was teaching me how to make model ships and put them in bottles," Tony said.

So Tony was the person Mr. Lang was teaching about ships in bottles. Allie wished she had known. This was hardly the time to ask about them, though. Allie wondered if there would be a good time ever again.

Tony went on. The thought of Mr. Lang

seemed to make him want to talk. "Gonna miss him. For one thing, I figured if I got good at models, I could sell them. But mostly, he made me think. Stretched my mind, you know? He believed in me. Always knew I'd get into college someday, even when my folks thought it was a silly idea and we didn't have the money."

"He's rich. How come he didn't just give you the money?" Jinx asked.

"Or lend it to you?" Allie added.

Tony snorted. "Mr. Lang never gives presents. You have to earn them. He saw what happened to his cousins when he gave them some money. It wasn't a pretty sight. 'The moochers,' he called them. For awhile there, they were always bugging him for handouts. They even tried to move into his house in Cincinnati for free. Now he makes them earn what he gives them."

"But he gives the island money," Allie said. "The library. The museum."

"Not outright," Tony explained. "We had to put up the building before he'd supply a fund for the books. And the house the museum is in? It was a wreck." Tony looked at his wrecked ship. He shrugged. "Oh, well. He'll be back in two years." Suddenly he seemed to remember who he was talking to. "I have to go back to work," he said abruptly. Just then they heard voices in the shop. "Besides, I have customers."

But it was just Owen and Daniel. "Hey, Tony," Owen said. "We can't get the mast to stay up. Do you have anything that might help?" Then he noticed who else was in the shop. He didn't smile. He stared at them through his thick glasses. As if they were bugs he'd never seen before.

"We didn't do it, Owen," Jinx said. "If

that's what you're thinking."

Owen glanced at Tony. But Tony wasn't looking at any of them. He'd picked up a socket wrench and was taking the outboard motor apart.

"Mom said you wouldn't do anything like that," Daniel said. "But I know how much you like to win."

"Not that way!" Allie cried. "I always play fair!"

Daniel shrugged. "She says to call. She wants to talk to you."

Owen stood next to Tony. "So what can we do about our mast?" he asked.

Jinx cut in. "Owen, how come you have two caps on your head?"

Daniel laughed. "I did that, and he didn't even notice." He swiped the New York Yankees cap off and tossed it at Tony. "I found it outside. You lose it?"

Tony let it drop. "Yankees? No way. I wear a Red Sox cap. Half the summer people are from New York, though. Customers always leave things around here. Put it in the lost and found." He pointed under the desk in the corner.

"Where did you say you found that?" Allie asked Daniel.

He shrugged. "Outside." He waved toward the back of the shop.

Jinx picked up the hat.

"Anything?" Allie asked.

"Like a name tag?" Jinx said. "That would be too easy. I'm going to check out back again. Maybe I'll notice something other than the splinters this time."

Allie didn't follow him out. Instead, she listened to Tony tell Owen and Daniel about rigging a mast. "I'd give you mine," Tony offered, "but it was wrecked." He didn't quite look at Allie. Owen and Daniel did, though. They stared at her with unsmiling faces.

Allie wanted to close her eyes. She wanted to go back to her boatyard. She'd attach the paddle wheel to the hull. She'd tighten the chain. She'd step the mast and attach the stays. And she'd forget everything else in her work.

But what was the point? She couldn't race. And it did no good to know she hadn't done anything wrong. People thought she was guilty. Even her brother.

Allie made a decision. She looked straight at Daniel. "You can have our rigging," she said.

"Really?" Owen asked.

"Everything is on the ground," Allie went on. "There's a mast, a little box it goes in, and some stays to hold it up."

Owen looked at Daniel. Daniel pretended to faint.

Explaining the steps helped keep Allie's mind clear. "Just screw the box near the bow of your boat. You can tie the stays to your railing."

Daniel yanked Owen's arm. "Quick. Let's get out of here before she changes her mind," he yelled.

"Thanks, Allie," Owen exclaimed as the two boys raced out the door.

Allie watched them go. Then she noticed Tony was watching her. "That was nice," he said. "Giving them your rigging."

Allie shrugged. "We can't use it anymore." Through the window she could see Jinx on his hands and knees, examining the ground. There had to be some clue out there, some proof, somewhere! They weren't guilty of anything. She looked Tony straight in the eye. "We really didn't do anything to your boat, Tony. We'll prove it to you."

"That'd be good," Tony said. "But, if you are innocent you'd better be careful." He pointed toward his splintered boat. "Whoever did that isn't playing games."

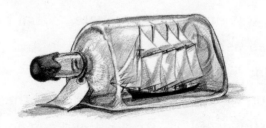

7

GUILTY UNTIL PROVEN INNOCENT

"Any clues?" Allie asked Jinx.

"About a million footprints," Jinx said. He stood up and brushed off his knees. "You know how popular this shop is."

Allie remembered the tracks she and Liz noticed. Had it only been that morning? "Did you notice any tracks that looked sort of like deer tracks?"

"Oval? And sharp edges?" Jinx asked. "Kind of like a heel?" He thought for a second. "Like this?" He pointed to a spot near the corner of the shop. "And here?" There was another by the gate. "What does that tell us?"

"Not much," Allie admitted.

"But we could look for more of these," Jinx suggested. "Around town. At other boatyards."

Allie groaned. "We'd be popular around other people's work areas."

Jinx kicked at a small stone stuck in the ground. "So you have a better idea?"

Allie shook her head. What else could they do? The day hung empty all around her. "I have to call home. That could change everything." Then she thought of something. "We could check out the museum. There might be other bottles with ships in them. Maybe seeing them would explain what's so special about the prize."

"Maybe. Maybe a ship in a bottle is really valuable." Jinx sounded doubtful. "I'd rather look for boot prints. Hey! We can go to the museum. But on the way, let's pass some other people's boatyards and look at the ground to see if there are any heel marks!"

"Okay. You look for clues along the way," Allie said. "I'll call home, then meet you at the museum."

Allie felt funny outside Tinkhams' store, making the call. It seemed like everyone was looking at her! She looked at the ground, then looked at the phone and concentrated on searching her pockets for coins.

Of course the line was busy.

Then she remembered how good it felt to look Tony in the eye. To say she hadn't done anything wrong, and to act that way. So when people stared at her, she stared back. She decided not to lie low. She'd face people. She might even talk to the other racers if she passed any between town and the museum.

She tried her call again, but the phone was still busy. She'd have to check in later. Maybe by the time later arrived, things would be okay.

Allie marched up School Street to Cross Street, passing Mr. Blake's house on the way.

Mr. Blake taught sixth grade at Ragged Island School. Of course he was building an entry for the race. And of course it wouldn't win. It wasn't built for speed. It was built to be original. He was making a Viking ship. It even had a dragon figurehead. It looked like the ships they had studied in his class.

Mr. Blake looked at her over the top of his glasses. "I just saw your partner in crime. You aren't in as much trouble as I heard, are you?" he asked.

Allie looked him straight in the eye. "We're in trouble," she admitted. "But we didn't do anything. All we've got to do is prove it."

Mr. Blake nodded. "That's what Jinx said. Well, you're good at proving things." He picked up his saw and started notching dragon teeth. "Good luck, then." Mr. Blake liked kids to solve their own problems.

"Thanks." Allie took a deep breath. That hadn't been so hard. She thought of the rest of the route to the museum. Who else would she pass?

Uh-oh! The Lang cottage. The Selfridges. Allie knew the Selfridges would recognize her right away. She didn't want to be chased again. She almost turned around.

But she hadn't done anything wrong. She hadn't. So she continued on her way.

She could hear hammering from behind the house. Good. They were busy. They wouldn't see her.

But just as she was passing by, the island delivery van rattled up. It shuddered to a stop next to her. Frank, the driver, leaned out the window and yelled. "Hey, Allie, do you know who's staying there?"

"The Selfridges." She had to yell over the sound of the noisy motor.

"That's the house, all right. I have a delivery for them," Frank said. "Look, this van is giving me trouble." He revved the engine a couple of times. "It'll stall if I get out." He opened his door and held out a package. "Would you take this up to them?"

Allie took the box. "You want me to take it in?" she asked.

But Frank didn't answer. He slammed the door. With a roar and a backfire, he drove off.

Allie looked down at the box.

```
TO:     ROBERT SELFRIDGE
        LANG COTTAGE
        RAGGED ISLAND, ME
FROM:   ACME ELECTRICAL SUPPLY
        100 FIRST STREET
        CINCINNATI, OH
```

She looked down the driveway. She could hear hammering still and the whine of an electric drill. They were working out back. She could leave it at the front door. That would be that. She squared her shoulders and headed toward the house.

She walked up the steps onto the porch. Should she leave the package here? Electrical stuff was expensive. What if someone took it? She'd be responsible. She'd be blamed again.

She knocked on the door. No answer. Maybe she could leave the package just inside the front door. They'd find it. So she opened the door and leaned over to set the package down.

Suddenly someone yelled, "Hey! What are you stealing?"

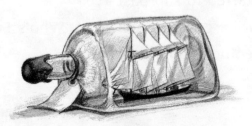

8
LOOKING FOR CLUES

Allie looked up. It was the big blond boy. Tye.
"I...Frank asked me to..."

"You again! Allie Davies, the boat wrecker!" he announced.

"I am not!" Allie felt the blood rush into her face.

"So now you're stealing stuff from our house." Tye glanced down at the box.

"I am not stealing anything." Allie worked hard to keep her voice from shaking.

"Frank asked me to deliver this package. And so I delivered it. And now I'm leaving." She started to slip past Tye.

But he grabbed her arm. "Who's Frank? How come you had this box?"

"Frank drives the delivery van. But his van's not running right. Let go!" She yanked free.

"You didn't drop it, did you?" Tye picked up the box and shook it. "I guess we lucked out. I hear you take great pleasure in wrecking boats."

Now Allie could look him in the eye. "I never, ever, would do such a thing. And I'll prove it!"

"You probably had such a pitiful boat," Tye sneered. "Destroying other boats was the only way you could win."

Allie straightened. "You are obviously not from around here," she said. "Everyone around here knows I have GREAT ideas."

"Ha!" Tye shouted back. "Everyone I've talked to says you wrecked one boat. And I know you tried to wreck ours. We saw you sneaking around."

What could Allie say? She wanted to run. But she made herself walk slowly down the steps, down the walkway, and back onto the road.

Now what?

These strangers from Ohio thought she'd wrecked Tony's boat. Maybe everyone believed that. How could she possibly prove she hadn't? Where should she go next?

The museum. She could hardly remember why she'd wanted to go to the museum. Slowly she worked it out in her mind. She wanted to see the ships in the bottles, to see if they were valuable. Maybe she'd be able to figure out why someone was trying so hard to get their hands on Mr. Lang's prize.

And Jinx would be there.

So Allie headed to the museum.

Ragged Island Museum was really an old house stuffed with island antiques. Most of it looked like junk, but there were three great displays. Every year the kids in Mr. Blake's class worked on one display until it was perfect.

Allie found Jinx examining a butter churn. "Find anything?" she asked. She'd decided not to talk about Tye.

Jinx listed what he'd learned. "Mr. Blake wished us luck. The Selfridges have a tar driveway. No tracks. Mark Mason was walking around barefoot, drinking juice. He said not to bother with his boat. He locks it up every night. He's planning to win."

"Frankly, I'm going to cheer for Daniel and Owen," Allie said. "What about the bottles?"

Jinx lifted the handle of the churn one more time. "I was waiting for you."

The ships in bottles were in the junky section.

"Maybe we could work on a ship-in-a-bottle display next year," Allie suggested.

"I'd rather do earliest islanders," Jinx said. "Arrowheads and stuff like that."

Mrs. Matthews took care of the museum. She wouldn't let them touch the bottles with ships in them. It wasn't as if she'd heard about Tony's wrecked boat. She didn't like anyone to touch anything, except in the "hands-on" display. She did lift the bottles down from their shelves. She held them in the not-very-bright light.

The first one was pretty simple. "Paper sails. One mast. Only a couple of lines," Allie observed.

"Oh, yes," Mrs. Matthews replied. "There are simple ones. First tries. But some are much more beautiful. Like this."

Mrs. Matthews held out another one. Even the bottle was amazing. One side was clear. The back had a crisscross pattern pressed into the glass.

And the ship? "Wow," Allie breathed. "Four masts. Look at all the rigging."

"Mr. Lang made this one." Mrs. Matthews said. "One of his earliest attempts. Yet still quite well done."

"It must be valuable," Jinx suggested.

"As a gift to our museum? It's priceless, of course. But you couldn't get that much money for one of these. It's for collecting, not a work of art," Mrs. Matthews explained.

Allie was still looking at all the details. "Look at the hatches. And the railings. He even named the ship."

"Oh, yes. Mr. Lang is always accurate." Mrs. Matthews sighed. "We'll miss him. But he'll be back. And until then..." She tapped her newspaper. "We always have his crossword puzzles."

"What next?" Jinx asked, as they stepped into the sunlight.

"Let's think about what we know and what we need to know," Allie said. She thought for a minute.

"We know nothing, and we need to know everything," Jinx said.

Allie laughed. "I'll say. We know someone broke into the Tinkhams' house. Then Tony's boat got wrecked."

"Do you think someone did that to have a better chance of winning?" Jinx asked.

"I don't know. We got blamed and kicked out, so there are two boats they don't have to beat." Allie broke off a branch of bayberry bush, crumpled the leaf, and sniffed. "Rats! I really wanted to race. Maybe we should go to Mrs. Tinkham and talk to her."

"What good would that do? Her mind's made up." Jinx sighed.

Allie shrugged. "We can at least try. I think it's good to face people. Usually."

They went to the Tinkhams' house. Lots of afternoons Mrs. Tinkham worked at home. Besides, they didn't want to go to the store. Too many people would be there.

Mrs. Tinkham wasn't in, but Drew was. "I started out weeding the garden, but mostly I'm weeding out broken glass," he said.

"From the break-in?" Jinx asked.

"I guess," Drew answered.

"Find anything?" Jinx sounded hopeful.

Drew shook his head.

"Boot marks? Like from cowboy boots?" Allie asked. She heard the phone ring inside.

"Nope. Nothing," Drew said.

The ringing continued. "Should we get that?" Allie asked.

Drew kept raking. "She isn't comfortable

101

letting me into the house anymore," he said. He shook his head. "It's a really weird feeling, being accused."

At last the ringing stopped with a click. Through the open window they heard Mrs. Tinkham's voice on her answering machine. She asked the caller to leave a message.

"Her message is longer than any caller's would be," Jinx said.

Allie hushed him. "Listen."

"This is Felix Partout, in Cincinnati." The voice on the phone spoke with an accent. "Forgive me for intruding. I thought you might need assistance in dealing with Mr. Lang's gift. Please call if I can be of any help. If you wish to reach me, my number is…"

Allie pulled a pencil out of her pocket. "Do either of you have a scrap of paper?" she whispered.

Neither boy did.

In that time they missed some of the message. They did hear the last part of a phone number. "291-2387."

She scratched the number in the freshly raked dirt.

"Did you get the area code?"

Neither boy had.

"I wonder what that's about?" Jinx said.

"The bottle? Could it be valuable?" Drew asked. He continued raking. He was careful to leave the numbers scratched in the dirt.

"But they couldn't sell it. It's a gift to the island," Allie said. She was looking around the yard. "It will be in the museum when it isn't a prize. There must be paper somewhere around here. Maybe in the garage? Just a scrap?"

"I'll check," Jinx said, "but I'll probably get arrested for stealing it."

Before Jinx could go, Drew exclaimed, "Hey, here's some paper." He got down on his hands and knees, reached deep under the peonies, and pulled out a piece of paper.

"Great," Allie said.

But before she could write the number, Jinx said, "Wait a minute. What is that?"

Allie opened it up.

"It's the tourist map. Streets. Major paths. Tourist sites. Stores and some people's houses. You know. These maps are just about everywhere."

"Even under a window of a house just broken into?"

Allie looked over the paper carefully. "No notes. No handwriting. No phone numbers."

"Still…" Jinx looked at the map. "The person who dropped it could have been the same person who broke in."

Allie agreed. She checked the paper one more time. Nothing. Then she wrote the seven digits. "What was his name?"

"Felix something," Drew remembered. "I have an idea. I'll hang around here and when Mrs. T. comes back, I'll listen again."

But that plan was changed the moment Mrs. Tinkham returned to the house. She didn't come alone. Tony and Owen walked on either side of her. Daniel came, too, riding his bike in circles around the others.

"What are you doing here?" Mrs. Tinkham asked abruptly.

"Raking and weeding," Drew said. "Isn't that what you hired me for?"

"We're helping," Jinx added quickly.

Mrs. Tinkham raised her eyebrows. "I'm sure you are."

"And we also came to talk to you," Allie added.

Mrs. Tinkham took a deep breath. "Well, I must say, you have good friends. A number of people have come to me, including these three." She waved her hand at Tony, Daniel, and Owen. "They reminded me a person is innocent of a crime until he or she is proven guilty." She looked sternly at Allie. "I am not dropping this matter," she said. "However, until I have more proof, I hereby reinstate your right to compete in the race."

Allie gasped. "Really? Oh, really?" She suddenly realized how empty she had been feeling. And now she felt so full. "Yikes, guys. We've got work to do!"

"Remember, you gave me your mast," Daniel said.

That stopped her for a second. "I remember," she said with dignity, "and still thank you. Thank you, everyone. But hurry, guys. We're going to have to work like crazy to get everything done in time!"

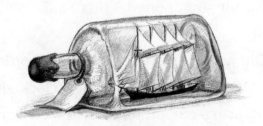

9

BOY OVERBOARD

They worked furiously, late into the afternoon. Allie and Liz had to stop at suppertime. Allie's mom was organizing a huge picnic for after the race. She wanted Allie to help at home. Liz was needed at the bed and breakfast. Drew and Jinx took turns going home for supper. Then they camped out next to the boat again.

They had no visitors.

Allie and Liz joined them as soon as it

was light enough to see. They brought breakfast.

"Nothing happened," Jinx said, waving a bagel.

"Okay, let's finish up here," Allie ordered. "Launching time will be eight o'clock sharp. Dad is using our motorboat to tow Daniel's boat around first. He'll come and tow ours after that. We won't have much time for a test run."

They had no time. Mr. Davies was waiting for them as they lugged the boat down the last fifty feet to the water.

"Good thing it's almost high tide," Mr. Davies observed. "That thing looks heavy."

"It is," grunted Drew.

"But seaworthy," Mr. Davies added. "Nice lines. Glad you are getting a chance to race." He passed out life jackets to everyone. "Now, who's coming with me and who's riding in the *Loon*?"

Allie and Liz climbed aboard the *Loon*. Drew and Jinx joined Mr. Davies on his boat.

It was a perfect day for the race. The sky was blue. The air was clear. There was some wind, but Allie was glad she'd thought of adding the pedal-paddle. That way, when they headed into the wind, they'd still get somewhere.

"Comfortable seat," Liz said.

111

"Sure you don't want to pedal during the race?" Allie asked. "Instead of Drew?"

"I have runner's muscles," Liz said. "Not biker's. And you know how strong Drew is."

Allie nodded. She checked the mast and stays. Not as good as the first set, but that was okay. Daniel and Owen were happy. And it was in part thanks to them that she could be in the race at all. They had stood up for her.

Soon they rounded the northern point protecting the harbor. There was no more time for thinking. Just about everyone on the entire island was either on the wharf or in the harbor. Boats, rafts, and piles of junk of all shapes and sizes filled the water. It was a good thing the ferry wasn't due!

Mr. Davies pulled alongside the *Titanic*. That was what Daniel and Owen called their boat. Mr. Davies shook his head over the name. "I wish you'd called your ship something else. You know what happened to the first one. You boys okay?" he asked.

Daniel saluted. Owen grinned.

Then Drew grabbed the tow rope and pulled the *Loon* alongside Mr. Davies's boat so he and Liz could change places.

Mr. Davies made sure everyone could see the markers of the race. "I'll drop Liz and Jinx at the wharf. Then I'll head near the south end of Harbor Island," he said. "All the motorboats will be out of your way. But we'll be ready to come and help at any sign of trouble. Okay?"

Owen and Daniel waved.

Allie gave a thumbs up. Then she remembered something. Something very important. She jammed her hand into the pocket of her shorts.

But it was the wrong pair of shorts. "Jinx. You've got to do something. You and Liz. Run to my house. Look in my room on the floor. You'll find some shorts there." Mr. Davies raised his eyebrows, but there wasn't any time to talk about messy rooms. "In the pocket, there's a paper with a phone number. Jinx knows. Remember?" Jinx nodded. "See if you can figure out who that guy is."

"Got it," Jinx said, just as Mr. Davies pushed his boat away.

So both little boats paddled toward the starting line.

Mr. Blake was already there in his Viking ship. The dragon on the front of his boat was winking. Mr. Selfridge drove his motorboat right by him, pulling Tye on their entry.

"Slow down," Mr. Blake yelled. But who could hear over all the noise in the harbor?

Allie scanned the scene. Owen and Daniel were the youngest racers. Some entries were little more than a sheet of plywood, with a lobster trap and a post in the middle. One young woman was just sitting on an old wooden lobster trap. Actually, she was floating in the water. The lobster trap was under her. Allie couldn't see her sail. The woman was laughing, though. She was wearing a wet suit. The harbor water was cold!

Not everyone was trying to win, Allie realized.

Some were desperate to, though. Tye Selfridge kept pushing to the front of the starting line. His boat had a strange shape. It was very narrow and had a small sail. Tye also had long oars. Maybe he was going to row his boat mostly. He would have to row fast in order to win.

Drew back-paddled with his oar to keep from being rammed. Allie, sitting behind Drew, tried to steer their boat away from the others. Then another boat bumped the *Loon* as it pushed past.

"Hey," Allie shouted.

"Look!" Drew said softly.

Mark Mason was sitting up proudly, head high, looking neither to the right nor the left. In one hand, he held the line coming down from a pulley at the top of his mast. He was ready to hoist his sail. In the other he held his tiller for steering. But what Drew had noticed was the pedal design. It was almost identical to Allie's. And he'd taken a lobster trap apart and put it together again in the shape of a chair.

Drew wasn't the only one who noticed.

Tye looked at Mark's boat and at the *Loon*. "Everyone knows how original you are," he sneered at Allie. "Right?"

Before Allie could react to that, Drew nudged her again. "Check out the name of his boat," he said quietly.

By now Mark's boat was squarely ahead of the *Loon*.

The name of Mark's boat was painted on the stern. *Maggie*.

"That was what Tony called his boat," Allie said. "What kind of shoes is he wearing?"

"Water slippers, same as me," Drew said.

"Of course," Allie said. "No one would wear boots with heels in a race like this."

Drew stopped paddling for a minute. "I know he wants to win the race. But why would he want to steal the bottle beforehand?"

"And he wouldn't have needed a map to find the Tinkhams' house," Allie added.

"Mark has spent a million summers here. He knows everyone."

"Shhh!" Drew warned. "They're saying something. Listen."

Mrs. Tinkham was in the bow of the starter's boat, shouting through a megaphone.

"What's she saying?" Daniel asked.

Someone shushed him. Someone else said, "She's going over the rules."

"It's about to start," Allie said. "Are you ready?"

Drew put down his oar and sat in the pedaling seat. Allie got ready to hoist the sail.

In the starter's boat, they saw Mrs. Tinkham stand. "On your mark," she yelled. At least everyone could hear that easily. "Get set." She raised her arm straight in the air. She was holding a starter's gun. She closed her eyes. She squeezed the trigger.

BANG!

They were off. Allie hoisted the sail and pulled it in. Drew pedaled like mad. Right away, the mass of boats separated into two groups. The rafts that were counting on the wind were mostly drifting. The boats with oars or paddles were making progress toward the first mark.

The *Loon* took an early lead. But the *Maggie* and the Selfridges' boat weren't far behind. Even Daniel and Owen, with two sets of oars, were in the front pack.

But soon Allie and Drew were too frantic to pay attention to anyone else. Allie, in the stern of the boat, was in charge of steering and sailing. Drew pedaled. He couldn't see a whole lot. The sail blocked his view.

Once they were under way, Drew could relax a little. During the first leg of the race, the wind was with them. Allie let her sail out and it caught the breeze. It was a big sail on a tall mast. Allie pulled ahead.

Once they rounded the first mark, Drew started to pedal hard. The wind was against them. The boats with only sails couldn't go in straight lines. They had to zigzag back and forth. Now Allie's job was to keep the sail out of Drew's way. Thanks to Drew's strong legs, they were still in the front of the pack.

Allie looked back. Tye Selfridge was right behind them, but it looked like the *Loon* was going to round the second buoy first.

Allie watched Tye's boat carefully. "How's he doing it?"

"Who? Doing what?" Drew huffed.

"Tye," she replied. His boat was narrow. It cut through the water cleanly. "He's rowing, but not very hard," she observed.

"Not as hard as you are pedaling. But he's really moving."

Drew couldn't look. He couldn't say more than "Huh!"

Allie turned her attention back to the sail.

The crowds on shore were cheering. People in nearby motorboats were rooting for their favorite boats. Drew was puffing. His face was bright red. Allie was getting ready to use the sail to pick up the breeze the moment they made a turn.

So she didn't notice exactly what happened next.

She did hear someone say, "Beep, beep." It sounded like Mark Mason.

She heard a thud.

She heard someone else yell, "Look out!" It sounded like Tye Selfridge.

When she looked around, she saw Mark's boat ramming its way past Tye's boat.

121

Tye's boat rammed into the *Loon*.

The *Loon* shuddered.

"Brace yourself," Allie yelled. Drew held on. Their boat, with the paddle underneath, was sturdy enough to take the jostling.

But Tye Selfridge's boat flipped right over. And Tye was thrashing around in the cold Maine ocean.

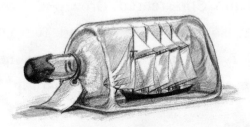

10
THE SNATCHED PRIZE

Allie felt torn in two at that moment. The *Loon* could win. Their sail was bigger than Mark's. Mark might pedal ahead for a while. But as soon as they got around the last buoy, she knew she could sail faster.

But she wasn't going to.

"He tipped over, Drew. We're coming about," she yelled.

"Ready," he called back.

Allie pushed the tiller away from her, let

out the sail, and turned the boat around. As they passed Mark's boat, he waved. Allie ignored him. She steered. Drew pedaled like crazy. As soon as they reached Tye, Drew grasped Tye's wrists. He hauled him up on the *Loon*, where they both lay gasping.

Then Allie's dad putted up alongside. He nodded. "Good job," he said. Allie knew she'd made the right decision. Mr. Davies said, "You all right, Tye?"

"That's cold water," Tye gasped.

"Fifty-nine degrees this time of year. Wouldn't last long without some kind of protection. Let's get you to shore so you can warm up."

Mr. Davies looked at Allie and Drew. "Are you going to finish the race?"

Allie and Drew looked up to see how the race was going. Most of the boats had rounded the last mark and were racing home. Allie felt funny about giving up. But Tye was shivering. "Maybe we could haul Tye's boat back to shore, so you could get Tye warmed up faster."

"Okay." Mr. Davies saluted them. "Hold on, Tye. We'll get you home."

It wasn't until they'd righted the Selfridge's boat that they saw how it had gone so fast with just Tye on it.

"They were cheating!" Drew exclaimed.

"A battery running an underwater propeller." Allie shook her head. The motor must have been in the box that Allie delivered to the Selfridges. "They wanted to win so much, they were willing to cheat."

"They weren't the only ones." Drew gestured toward the wharf. "Look at Mark Mason, pedaling like a king."

"He didn't cheat," said Allie.

"Maybe not. He stole our pedal-paddle design though. And did you see his lobster trap seat? It was identical to ours."

Allie looked at Drew. "Do you think he spied on us? That night, when we all chased after that sound?"

Drew was tying Tye's boat to the *Loon*.

"Maybe. Maybe he took the pry bar at the same time. Mark really wanted to win. He always has to win. And he was especially mad at Tony for stealing *Maggie* from him. But we have no proof."

"You know," Allie said slowly. "All this time I've been thinking that one person was behind everything. One person broke into Mrs. Tinkham's. The same person wrecked Tony's boat. But what if two people were involved?"

Drew looked confused. "Mark and the Selfridges are working together?"

"I don't know. The Selfridges wanted to win, too. Enough to cheat. But I still don't know why." Allie sailed slowly toward the shore. They watched Mark pedal across the line first.

"Well, he did it. He won," Drew said.

"And look! Daniel and Owen are coming

in second," Allie yelled. "They'll be so excited." She tried not to feel too jealous. "At least it was a good mast."

"Let's get back fast," Drew said. "The prize gets presented as soon as everyone is in safely."

It didn't take long to get back to shore, even dragging the Selfridges' boat. Liz and Jinx had run down onto the beach to greet them.

"You were miles ahead," Jinx said. "The *Loon* would have won, easy. What happened to Tye's boat?"

"You couldn't see what happened?" Drew asked.

"We saw Tye in the water," Liz said. "You rescued him."

"Mark bumped into him," Allie said.

"And us," Drew added.

"And kept going?" Liz was furious. "Then

he didn't win. It shouldn't count!"

Allie shrugged. "You were watching, and you didn't see it happen. We have no proof."

"Tye could tell Mrs. Tinkham. He was doing great when Mark wrecked it all," Liz insisted.

Allie shook her head. "He's not going to say anything. The Selfridge's were using an electric motor. They were cheating too."

Suddenly Allie remembered Liz and Jinx hadn't just watched the race. They had made a phone call. "Wait a minute! What did you find out?" Allie asked.

"We tried the number, but it wasn't in this state," Jinx said. "So then we looked in the front of the phone book."

"There were about a million area codes," Liz added. "But then Jinx got a brilliant idea."

"We tried the area code for the Cincinnati

area," he said. "And bingo!"

"Felix Partout has a jewelry business in Ohio," Liz said.

"Did you talk to him?" Allie asked.

Liz shook her head. "It would have taken too long. As soon as we found out, we raced back here."

"Mrs. Tinkham will present the bottle to the winner as soon as everyone's in," Jinx said. "That's about now."

Allie looked at the course. Even the smiling woman in the lobster trap had made it around the course. Now Allie could see the sail. It was about the size of a handkerchief.

She looked around the wharf. There were the Selfridges. It looked like they were yelling at Tye. And Tye must have been injured. He was leaning on one of his oars. Then she noticed Daniel and Owen and waved them over. Owen's sister, Lauren, came too. "Where's Mark?" Allie asked her.

"He went to get changed," Lauren said. She tossed her hair. "He wants to look just so for the photographers. He probably thinks if he gets his picture in the paper, Maggie will come back to him."

Daniel confided to Allie, "We were going to stop, too. But Owen doesn't see so well, and by the time I explained what had happened, you were already there."

"I'm glad one Davies boat won," Allie assured him.

"Here he comes now," Lauren called out.

Mark Mason strode down the wharf as if it all belonged to him. A few townspeople cheered. Some clapped. He smiled, then paused briefly by Allie and her friends. "Where's old Tony? Couldn't stand to watch me win?" He didn't wait for an answer, but

walked on with a wave.

"He walks as though he wants to leave all us little people in the dust," Liz said.

"Speaking of dust," Jinx said, "look down."

There, in the dusty gravel, were his footprints.

Oval. With sharp edges.

Allie said, "Cowboy boots."

"You know what," Owen said. He squinted after Mark. "He doesn't have a hat."

Liz smiled. "You're right. He doesn't."

"But he always wears a baseball hat. We fight about it," said Owen.

"You fight?" Drew asked.

"Yeah. He's for the Yankees," Owen explained.

Allie and Jinx looked at each other.

"Hey, bud," Jinx said to Daniel. "You know that hat you found?"

Daniel nodded. "The one we put in the lost and found?"

"You're fastest, Liz," Jinx said. "Go for it! I'm going to stop Mrs. T."

"You'll probably need a bulldozer," Drew said, but everyone had left except Allie.

"There's still something not right about

this," Allie muttered to Drew. "Mark could have taken my pry bar when he sneaked up on us working on the *Loon*. He certainly could have wrecked Tony's boat. But he couldn't have done everything."

"Like the break-in?" Drew replied.

"Mark didn't want the bottle," Allie reminded him. "He wanted to win. And what about the map you found? Mark has lived here all his life. In summer, at least. He knows the island almost as well as we do. So he wouldn't need a map."

"Ladies and gentlemen. Boys and girls," Mrs. Tinkham announced in her loudest public voice. Jinx was standing beside her with a scowl on his face.

"I guess Jinx didn't have much luck," Drew said.

"Welcome to the first ever Tyler Selfridge Lang Around the Harbor Lobster Trap Race."

134

"Wait a minute! Tyler Selfridge!" Allie exclaimed.

"He must be related," Drew said.

Allie closed her eyes, trying to grasp a nearly forgotten memory. "Gramp or Tony— someone said something about Mr. Lang's cousins. Where were we? Oh!" she opened her eyes. "You weren't there. Tony knew. The cousins were moochers, he said."

"Mooching at his house?"

"Not on the island. His other house. The one in Cincinnati. Remember, these Selfridges had Ohio license plates. Gramp said relatives were renting that house, right? And Tony said the moochers had to earn what he gave them. They had to pay rent. So the Selfridges are the moochers!"

"Do you think they found something about the prize for this race while they were staying at Mr. Lang's house?" Drew asked.

"Maybe Mr. Partout called there first!" Allie guessed. "Let's get closer. This isn't over yet."

Liz and Daniel were already back. Jinx was still trying, politely, to interrupt Mrs. Tinkham.

At last she paused long enough to say, "For goodness sake, what is it, Jinx?"

He said something to her quietly. She asked Daniel a question. Then Owen. Allie was amazed. She'd never known Mrs. Tinkham to speak quietly before.

Allie and Drew edged closer. Now they heard her ask Mark Mason, "You hardly look dressed without your hat. Is this yours?"

"Yeah! I misplaced it the other day. Thanks so much," Mark said.

"Now, Daniel. Would you mind telling Mark where you found the hat?"

"Under Tony's wrecked boat," Daniel said.

Allie had never seen such a tan face turn pale so quickly.

"I...This couldn't be..." Mark stammered.

"And Daniel tells me tracks like the ones your cowboy boots make were found, let's see...at his sister's boatyard and at Tony's house."

Mark didn't have much to say.

Mrs. Tinkham did. "I also notice your boat design is similar to Allie's."

Mark was looking down at his feet.

"Now, this is not a court of law. I could call Sheriff Greenwood in." Mark looked up suddenly, with horror in his eyes.

"Or you could quietly disappear right now," she said, "and write a few letters of apology this afternoon. Wanting to win is not bad in itself as long as you don't want to win too much."

Allie knew exactly what she meant.

Mark slunk away, but not before he saw the passengers getting off the ferry. He saw Maggie climb off smiling and rush into Tony's arms. That's when Mark disappeared in a hurry.

Mrs. Tinkham raised her public voice again. "Now it is time to present the prize to the winners of the first annual Around the Harbor Lobster Trap Race! The winners are two hardworking, clever boys: Owen McBride and Daniel Davies!"

The crowd erupted in cheers. Allie was watching the bottle so carefully she hardly felt any regret. Daniel got to keep the bottle for three and a half days. Since her mast helped him win, maybe he'd let her examine the bottle. She might be able to figure out how the ship got inside.

But Drew elbowed her, and as she looked up she realized Mr. Selfridge was edging closer. Much closer.

As Owen clutched the bottle and grinned, and as Daniel bowed to his audience, Mr. Selfridge snatched the bottle out of Owen's grasp.

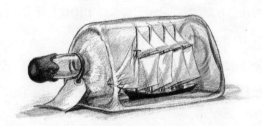

11

WINNER AT LAST

Jinx was quickest.

"Don't let him get away," he yelled.

Drew and Liz were close by. In a blink, Mr. Selfridge found he was surrounded.

"Lois," he cried. He held the bottle over his head. His wife was on the edge of the crowd. Once she was ready, he tossed it in a gentle arc over everyone's head, right toward her.

Mrs. Selfridge was well out of reach of

Allie or any of her friends.

Then Tye called out, "I've got it!" He lifted the paddle he was clutching and stopped the bottle with a clunk.

It fell almost in front of Allie. She snatched at it, desperate to break its fall.

Suddenly, she was standing with the bottle in her hand.

She checked it carefully. It was okay. No, it was better than okay. It was perfect. She had never seen such a perfect ship, even full sized. Everything was exact on it—perfect sails, perfect rigging.

It was a four-masted schooner. Every detail was exact, right down to its name, painted in tiny letters: *Mackerel Bay*.

Suddenly, Allie knew the answer to the mystery of the ship in the bottle.

"I know where Mr. Lang's gift is," she shouted. "The clue is on the tag. Listen: 'To the people of Ragged Island, a jewel in the middle of Mackerel Bay.' And look! The ship in the bottle is called *Mackerel Bay*!"

Even Mrs. Tinkham believed Allie this time. "But how will we get it out?" she worried. "The bottle itself is worth something. It would be a shame to break it."

Still, she seemed ready to. Allie was glad she had hold of it.

But by this time, Tony showed up, his arm around Maggie. He shrugged. "No problem. I have exactly the tool."

"I'll get it," Liz offered. So once again she raced up to her uncle's fix-it shop. She found the long-handled tweezers exactly where Tony told her they would be.

And carefully, carefully, Tony uncorked the bottle. He reached into the narrow mouth with his tweezers. He gently plucked at a hatch cover and pulled out a small packet.

Allie found she was holding her breath. When Tony gently set the packet in Mrs. Tinkham's outstretched hand, and Allie heard the whole town sigh, she realized everyone had stopped breathing.

"For the scholarship fund," Mrs. Tinkham read. She opened the envelope and tipped out a perfect diamond.

The people on the wharf broke into applause—the loudest of the day.

Mrs. Tinkham said softly, "Well, there are certainly people on this island who will deserve that scholarship!" Her fingers closed around the brilliant jewel. She beamed at her audience. "I'm going to put this in a safe place. A really safe place! And you are all invited to the international picnic in the school yard."

It was only as they walked up toward the school that Allie asked, "What happened to the Selfridges?"

"They tried to sneak away," Liz said.

"I don't think they'll get very far," Jinx said. "I saw Mrs. Tinkham talking to Sheriff Greenwood."

"And Mark?" Drew asked.

"Maybe he'll find a job off-island for the rest of the summer," Jinx suggested.

Allie listened to her friends talk about what had happened. She listened to passing islanders discuss the jewel. She heard some of the racers compare boat designs. "Hey, you know what?" she told her friends. "I have a great idea for next year's race."

Drew groaned. Liz laughed.

"Oh my aching bones," Jinx complained.

And even though Allie hadn't won a thing, she still felt like a winner.

About the Author

Emily Herman lives on an island in Maine with her husband, Dave, and her two children, Ben and Joanna. When she is not writing or teaching, she likes to climb mountains, take pictures, sail and canoe, quilt, and work in her gardens. She has written a number of books including *The Missing Fossil Mystery* and *Stones from the Muse.*